Carrot Soup

For Emily and Josh

Margaret K. McElderry Books

An imprint of Simon & Schuster Children's Publishing Division

1230 Avenue of the Americas, New York, New York 10020

Book design by Lee Wade

The text for this book is set in Golden Cockerel ITC.

The illustrations for this book are rendered in pencil and watercolor on Arches cold press watercolor paper.

Manufactured in China

4 6 8 10 9 7 5 3

Library of Congress Cataloging-in-Publication Data

Segal, John.

Carrot soup / John Segal.—1st ed.

p. cm.

Summary: After working hard on his garden all spring and summer,
Rabbit looks forward to harvest time when he can make soup, but every carrot disappears and Rabbit
must find out who has taken them. Includes a recipe for carrot soup.

ISBN-13: 978-0-689-87702-5

ISBN-10: 0-689-87702-1 (hardcover)

[1. Carrots—Fiction. 2. Lost and found possessions—Fiction. 3. Rabbits—Fiction.
4. Animals—Fiction. 5. Gardening—Fiction.] I. Title.

PZ7.S45258Car 2006

[E]—dc22

2004016963

Carrot Soup

WRITTEN and ILLUSTRATED by

JOHN SEGAL

Margaret K. McElderry Books

New York o LONDON o TORONTO o Sydney

It was spring—Rabbit's favorite season!

It was time to plan the garden, order
carrot seeds, and look forward to enjoying his
favorite food—carrot soup.

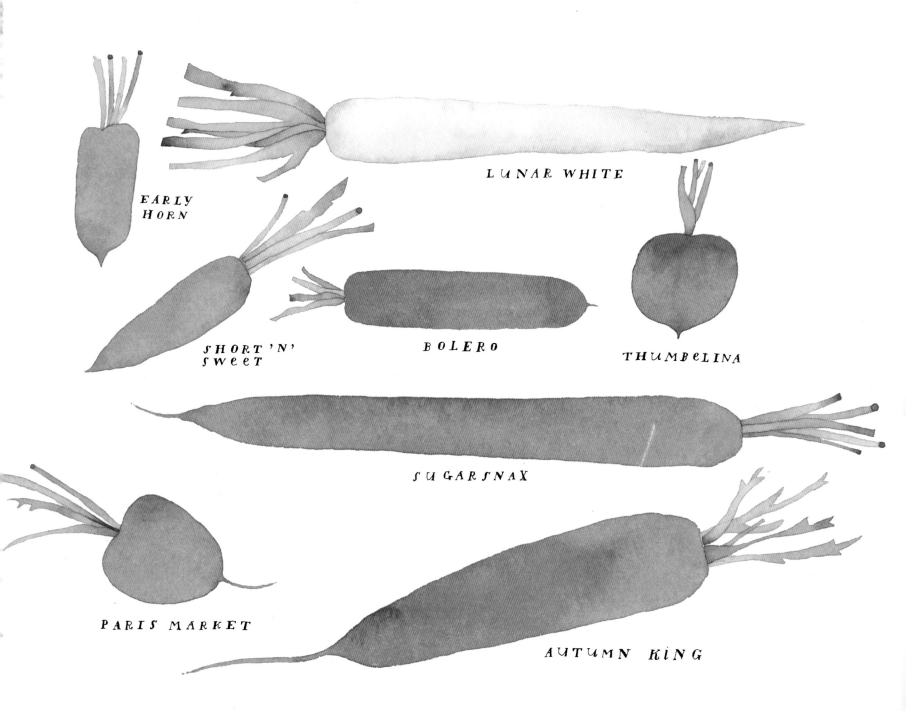

EARLY
HORN

LUNAR WHITE

SHORT 'N'
SWEET

BOLERO

THUMBELINA

SUGARSNAX

PARIS MARKET

AUTUMN KING

Rabbit plowed

and planted.

Rabbit watered

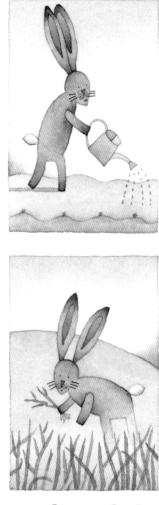

and weeded.

He waited . . .

and waited . . .

and waited . . .

. . . until finally it was time to pick the carrots.

Rabbit gathered his tools and his wheelbarrow, and

he

went.

But something was terribly wrong at the carrot patch.

Rabbit
looked up.

Rabbit
looked down.

He looked over
and under

and inside
and out.

Rabbit saw

roots   and rocks   and dirt   and mud.

But what Rabbit did not see were . . .

. . . carrots!

There were

NO CARROTS.

They were gone!

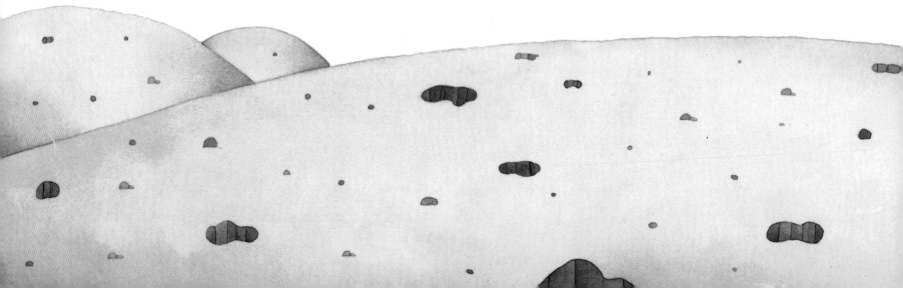

Rabbit went to see Mole.
"Mole, have you seen my
carrots?" Rabbit asked.

"Someone has stolen
my carrots!"

And Mole replied, "Rabbit, you know I don't see very well.
Why don't you ask Dog?"

"Dog, someone has taken all of my carrots!" said Rabbit.

"Have you seen them?"

"I don't care much for carrots," said Dog.
"Why don't you ask Cat?"

"Cat, I was hoping to have carrot soup tonight, but my carrots have disappeared!" said Rabbit.

"Have you seen them?"

"Carrots?" asked Cat.
"Why would I be interested in your carrots?
Perhaps Duck knows something about carrots."

Rabbit asked Duck,

"Have you
seen my
carrots?"

"I prefer fish to carrots," said Duck.

"Pig will eat anything, though. Maybe he has seen your carrots."

But Pig was nowhere to be found.

No carrot soup tonight,
thought Rabbit sadly.

Discouraged and disappointed,

Rabbit went home.

RABBIT'S FAVORITE CARROT SOUP

(Rabbit says, "Be sure to have a grown-up help you make this soup!")

2 pounds carrots—washed, peeled, and shredded

4 14-ounce cans chicken broth

2 stalks celery, chopped

1 large onion, chopped

1/4 cup butter

salt and pepper

5 sprigs fresh dill or parsley, minced

1. Sauté the onion and celery in butter in a large covered pot until tender. Add the shredded carrots and chicken broth. Bring to a boil.

2. Reduce heat and simmer with the pot covered for about a half hour.

3. Let cool slightly. Puree the mixture in a blender or food processor until smooth.

4. Add salt and pepper to taste. Add dill or parsley. Serve.

Serves 10.

Delicious!